DC COMICS™
SUPER HEROES

SUPERMAN™

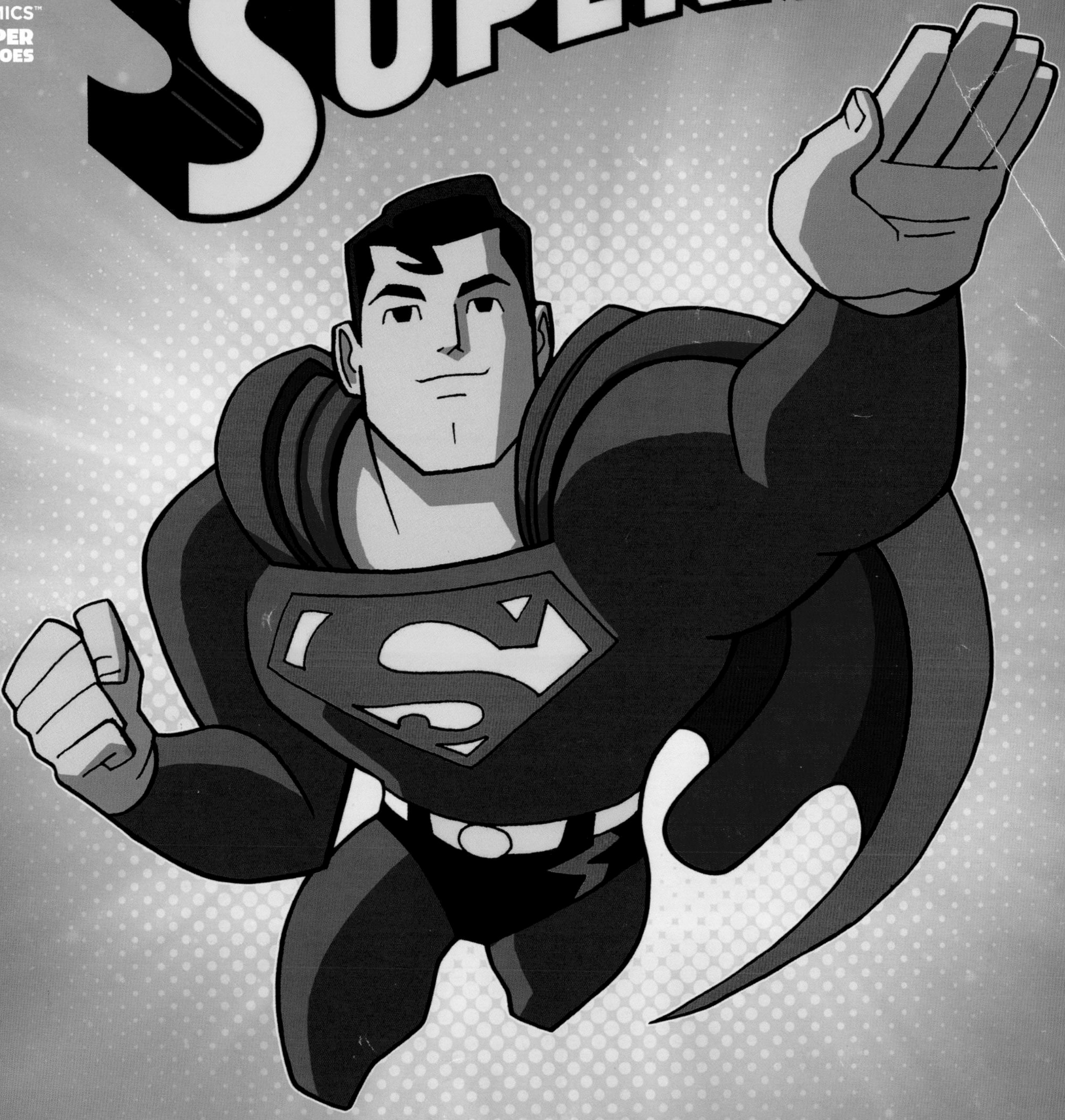

AN ORIGIN STORY

STONE ARCH BOOKS
A CAPSTONE IMPRINT

Published by Stone Arch Books in 2015
A Capstone Imprint
1710 Roe Crest Drive
North Mankato, MN 56003
www.capstonepub.com

STAR34387

Cataloging-in-Publication Data is available at the Library of Congress website
ISBN: 978-1-4342-9728-0 (library binding)
ISBN: 978-1-4342-9732-7 (paperback)
ISBN: 978-1-4965-0162-2 (eBook)

Summary: One day, an alien orphan crash-lands on Earth and is adopted by a human couple, the Kents. Many years later, that little baby becomes Superman, protector of Earth! But how did the Man of Steel go from orphan to super hero? Experience Clark Kent's incredible journey in this action-packed chapter book for early readers featuring vibrant art by DC Comics illustrators.

Contributing artists: Tim Levins, Dan Schoening, Erik Doescher, Mike DeCarlo, Lee Loughridge and Ethen Beavers
Designed by Hilary Wacholz

Printed in the United States of America in North Mankato, Minnesota
042015   008881R

DC COMICS™ SUPER HEROES

AN ORIGIN STORY

WRITTEN BY
MATTHEW K. MANNING

ILLUSTRATED BY
LUCIANO VECCHIO

SUPERMAN CREATED BY
JERRY SIEGEL AND JOE SHUSTER
BY SPECIAL ARRANGEMENT WITH
THE JERRY SIEGEL FAMILY

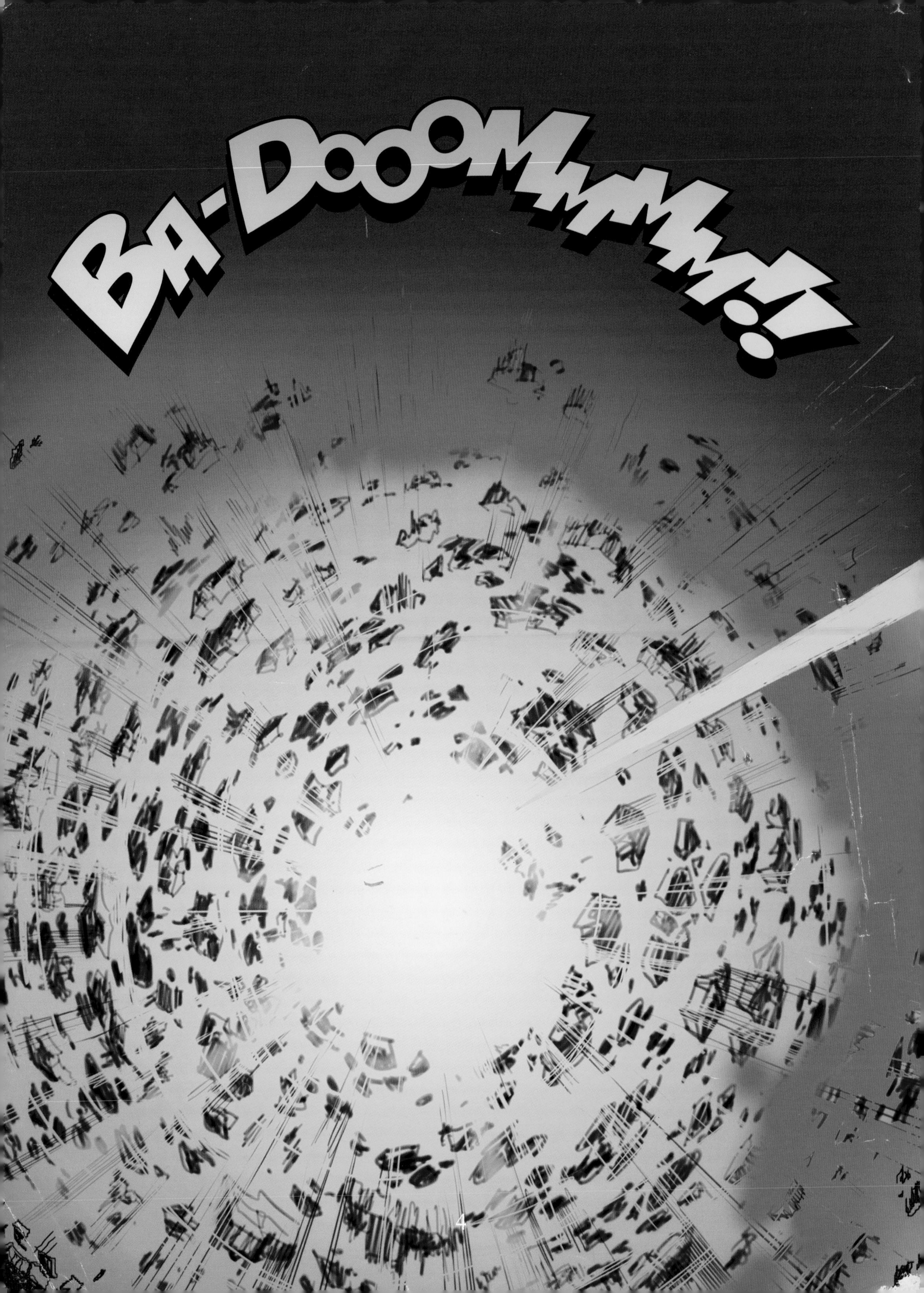
BA-DOOOMMMM!!

They say the universe began with a big bang.

The same can be said for the life of the boy who would become known as Superman.

In a distant part of the universe, the planet Krypton is destroyed. A lone rocket ship survives the explosion.

On board this tiny spacecraft is a single passenger. A little baby named Kal-El.

Kal holds tight to the blanket his mother gave him. He dreams of being held in her arms.

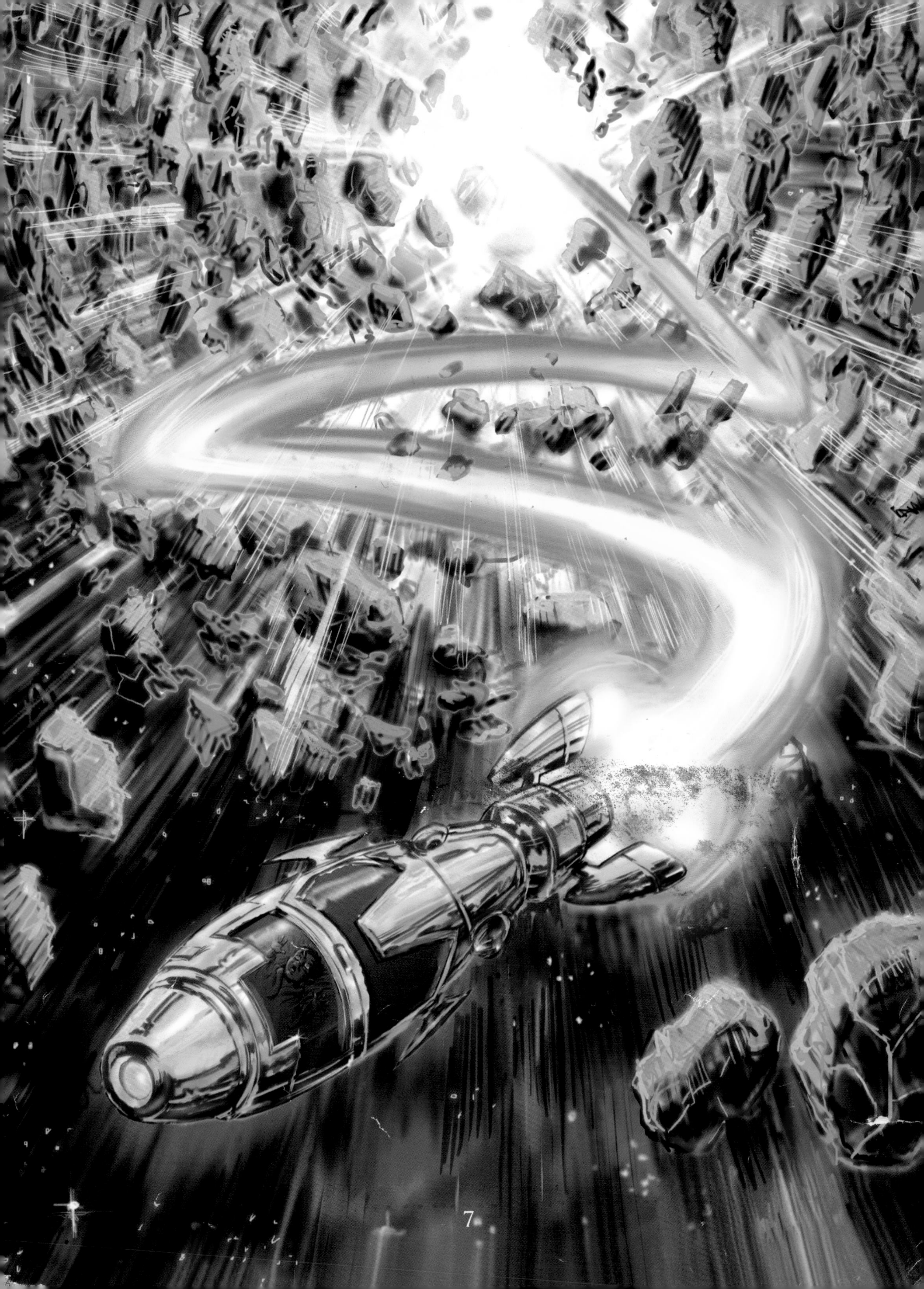

When the rocket ship stops moving, the baby wakes up.

Cold air fills his lungs. He opens his eyes. Two friendly faces are looking back at him.

"We're keeping him, Jonathan," says the woman. Kal-El likes her face. Her smile is warm. It is just like his mother's smile.

“Oh, Martha,” says the man next to her. “We don’t know anything about this child. We can’t just take him.”

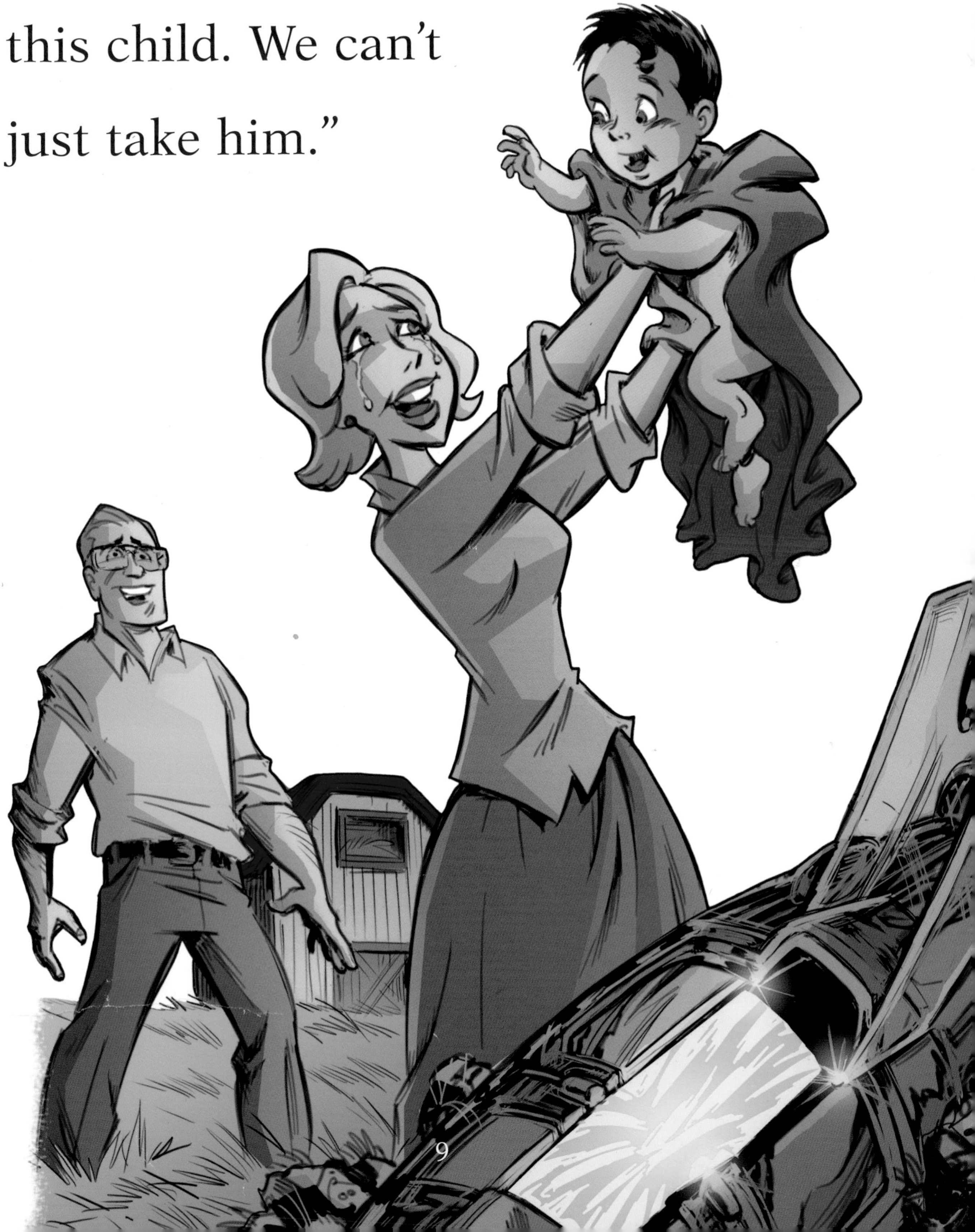

Kal-El reaches out. He wraps
his hand around the man's finger.

Now Jonathan is smiling, too.

"What do you think of the name
Clark?" asks the woman.

With his eyes open wide, Kal-El
smiles at the woman.

Sixteen years later, Kal-El is still
smiling.

His friends call him Clark now. He
leads a normal life in the town of
Smallville, Kansas. Or at least he did
until one fateful day.

Lana Lang tries to recite this week's poem from memory in front of the class. At the same time, Clark wonders what the school is serving for lunch.

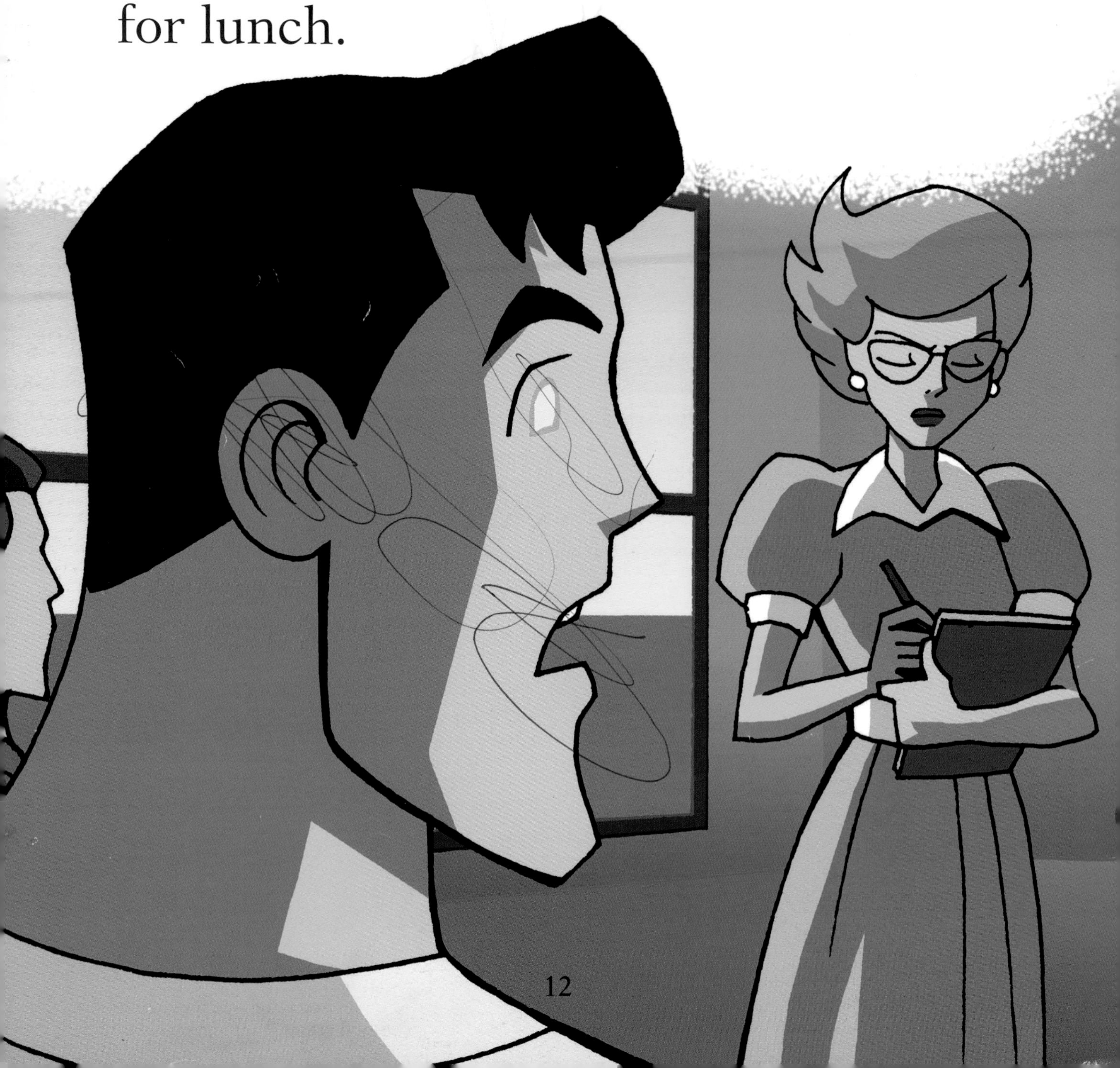

Suddenly, he realizes that he's looking right through the wall into the cafeteria.

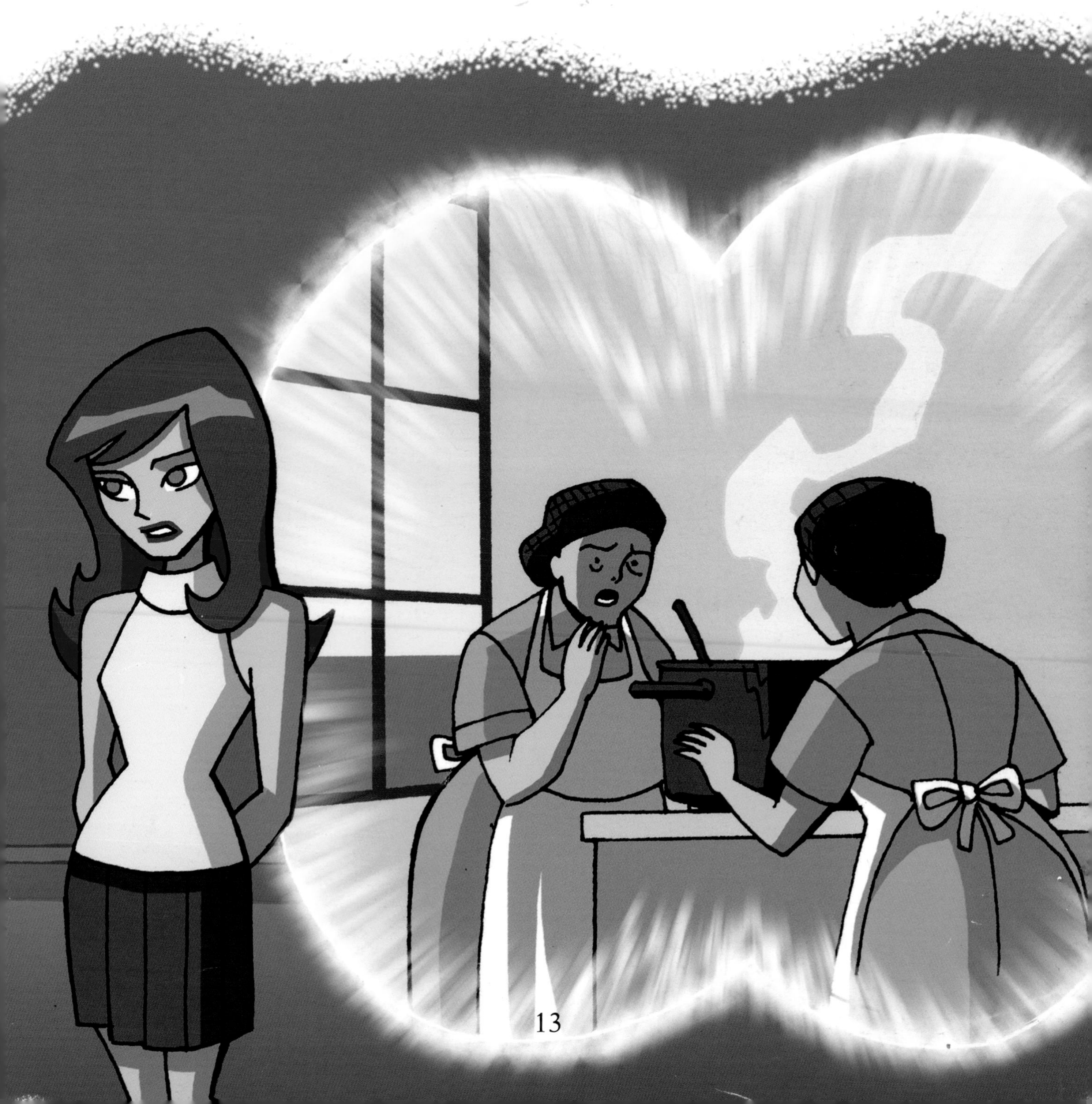

"I think I lost my keys," says Mrs. Owens.

Mrs. Lancaster sighs. "Again, Gladys?" she asks. "I'll help you look for them."

Clark is seeing into the cafeteria. He can hear the cook's conversation. It's like they are in the room with him!

"Are you okay, Clark?" asks Mrs. Brown.

Clark nods his head. But he knows that he is anything but okay.

Later, the old barn door slowly creaks open.

Jonathan and Martha Kent glance at each other. Then they walk inside.

Clark's parents seemed worried ever since Clark got home from school that day. He had told them what happened at school. He had lots of questions for them.

Now, Clark would get some answers.

Jonathan lifts up the dusty lid to a wooden box. Clark had never paid much attention to the box before today.

Inside is a metal ship. It looks familiar to Clark. But he doesn't know why.

"This is where we found you," says Jonathan.

Clark doesn't know what to think.

Then his father hands Clark a small box. It was the only thing they had found inside the ship with Clark all those years ago.

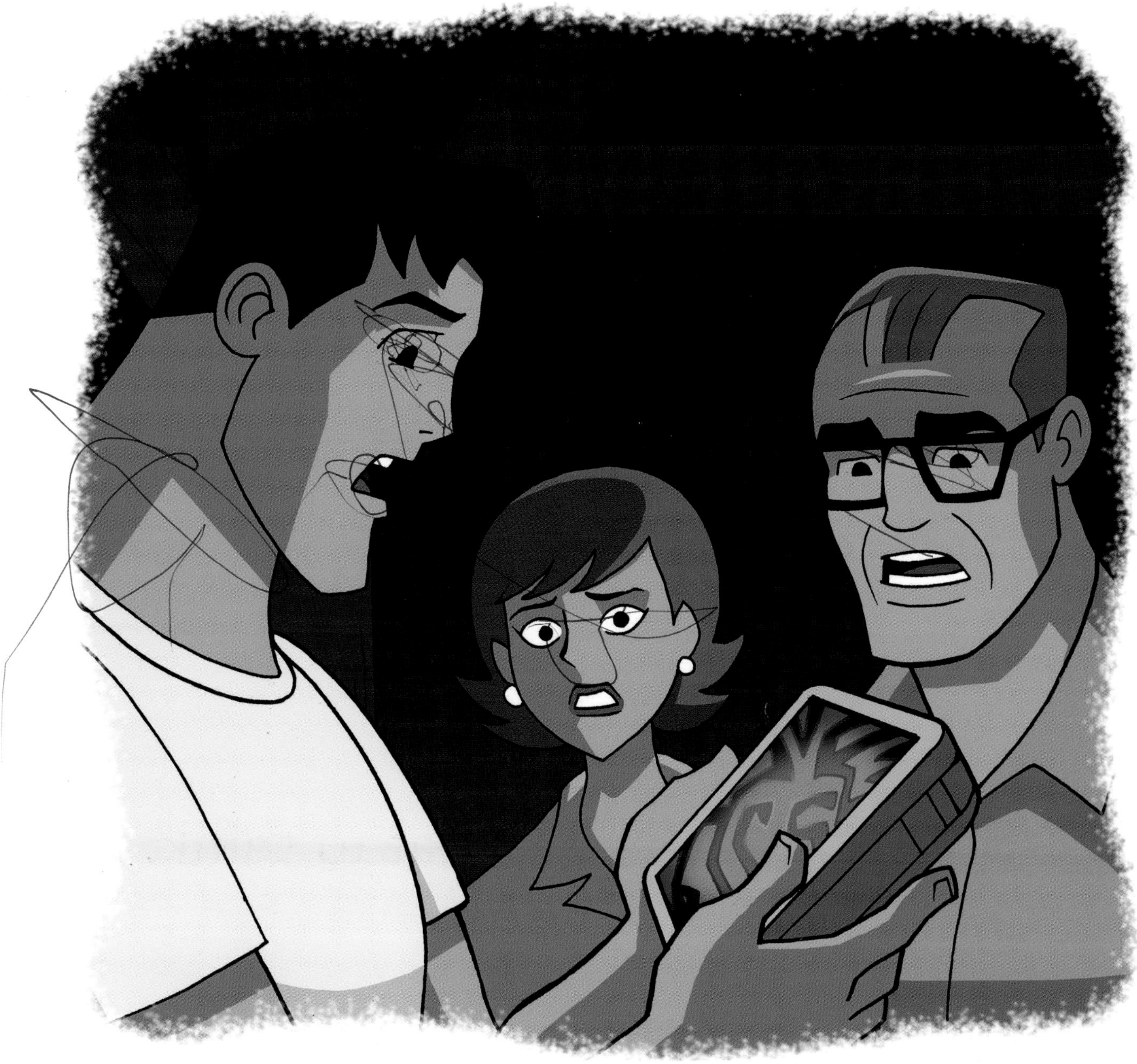

Jonathan and Martha never could get the box to work. But in Clark's hands, the device lights up.

Something that looks like an "S"
fills the screen.

Light from the object shines on Clark's forehead.

The world falls away around Clark. He no longer sees Smallville.

Instead, he sees the planet Krypton around him.

Clark watches as a man named Jor-El hands a young infant to his wife, Lara.

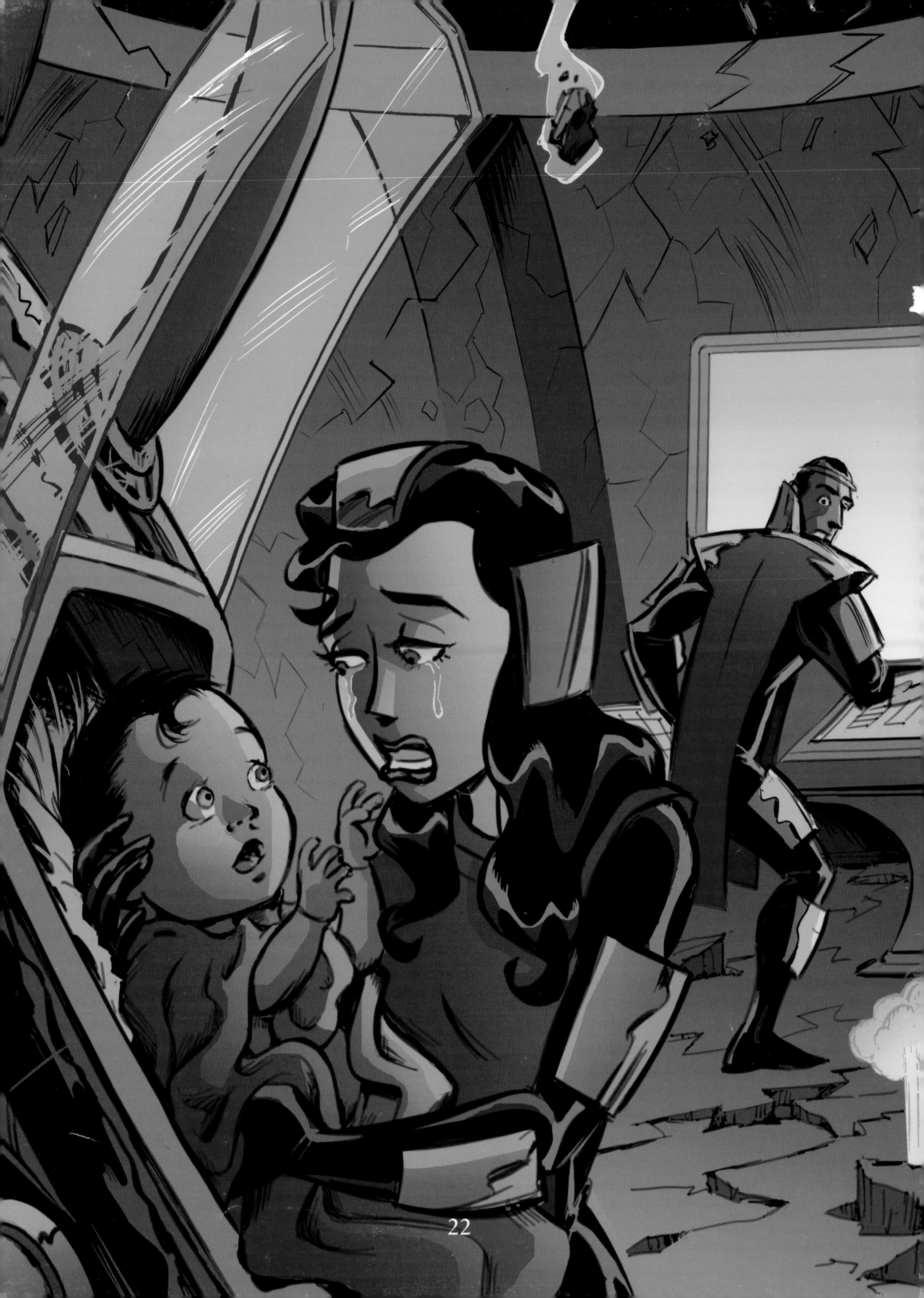

Lara is crying. She is hugging the child tightly.

Beneath their feet, the ground begins to shake. They both know they must say good-bye to their son.

If baby Kal-El is to survive, he must leave Krypton. Jor-El and Lara place him in a rocket ship.

The ship takes off just as the world around it explodes.

Clark opens his eyes. Small back.

Jonathan and Martha Kent watch as Clark comes back into focus.

Clark looks at them. Then he runs out of the barn. And he keeps on running.

Clark doesn't notice that he is moving faster than normal.

Soon he is dashing through the fields with super-speed!

He doesn't even notice when his feet lift off the ground.

He doesn't notice that he's flying until it's already happening.

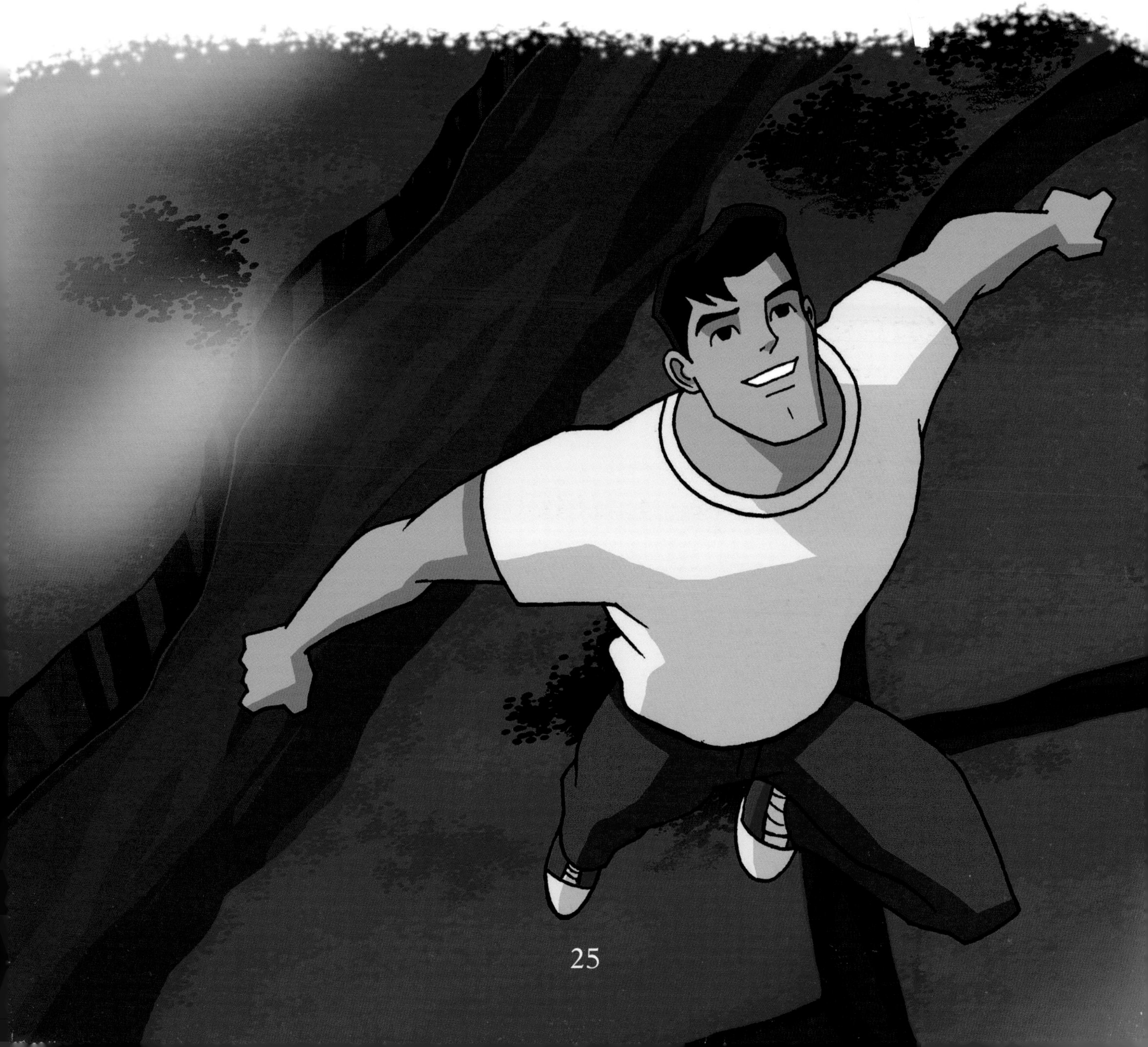

A short while later, Clark returns to the family barn.

Clark lands on the ground.

For a long moment, he and his parents just stare at each other.

Then Clark hugs them. Now he knows who he is. He knows where he came from. And he knows what he has to do on planet Earth.

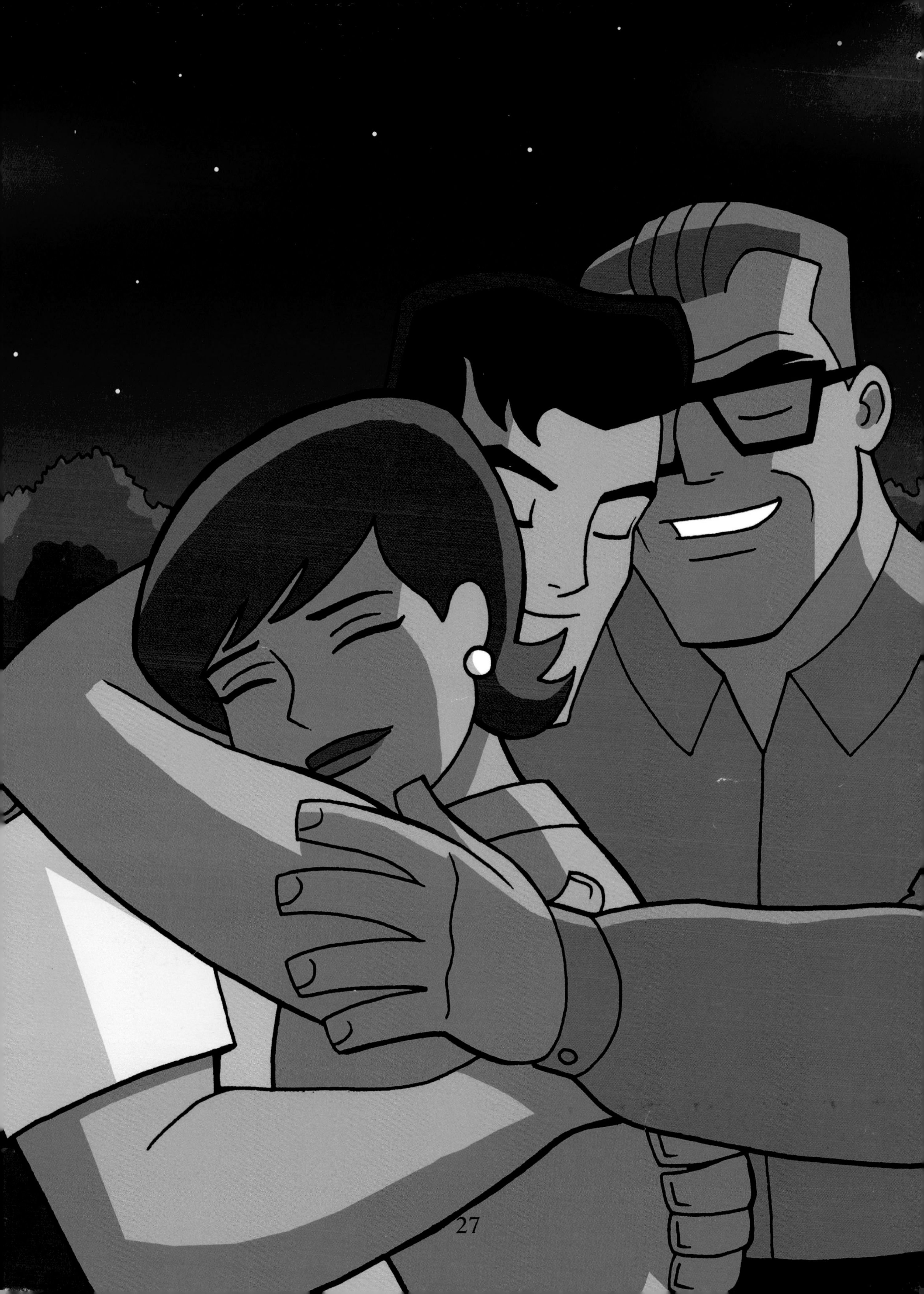

Years later, Clark rides a train. His eyes are closed when he hears the conductor.

"Last stop!" the man shouts. "Metropolis! Everybody off!"

Clark adjusts his hat as he steps off the train. He looks around at his new home.

Clark left Smallville to come to Metropolis.

The giant city is very different from his small hometown. It is like no other place he has visited before. But Clark could not go sightseeing just yet.

Today is Clark's first day at his new job. He is a reporter for the famous newspaper known as the *Daily Planet*.

Everyone is so busy that they hardly notice Clark at the *Daily Planet*.

Clark's boss, Perry White, is too busy to hand Clark his first assignment.

Instead, Perry introduces him to his new partner, Lois Lane.

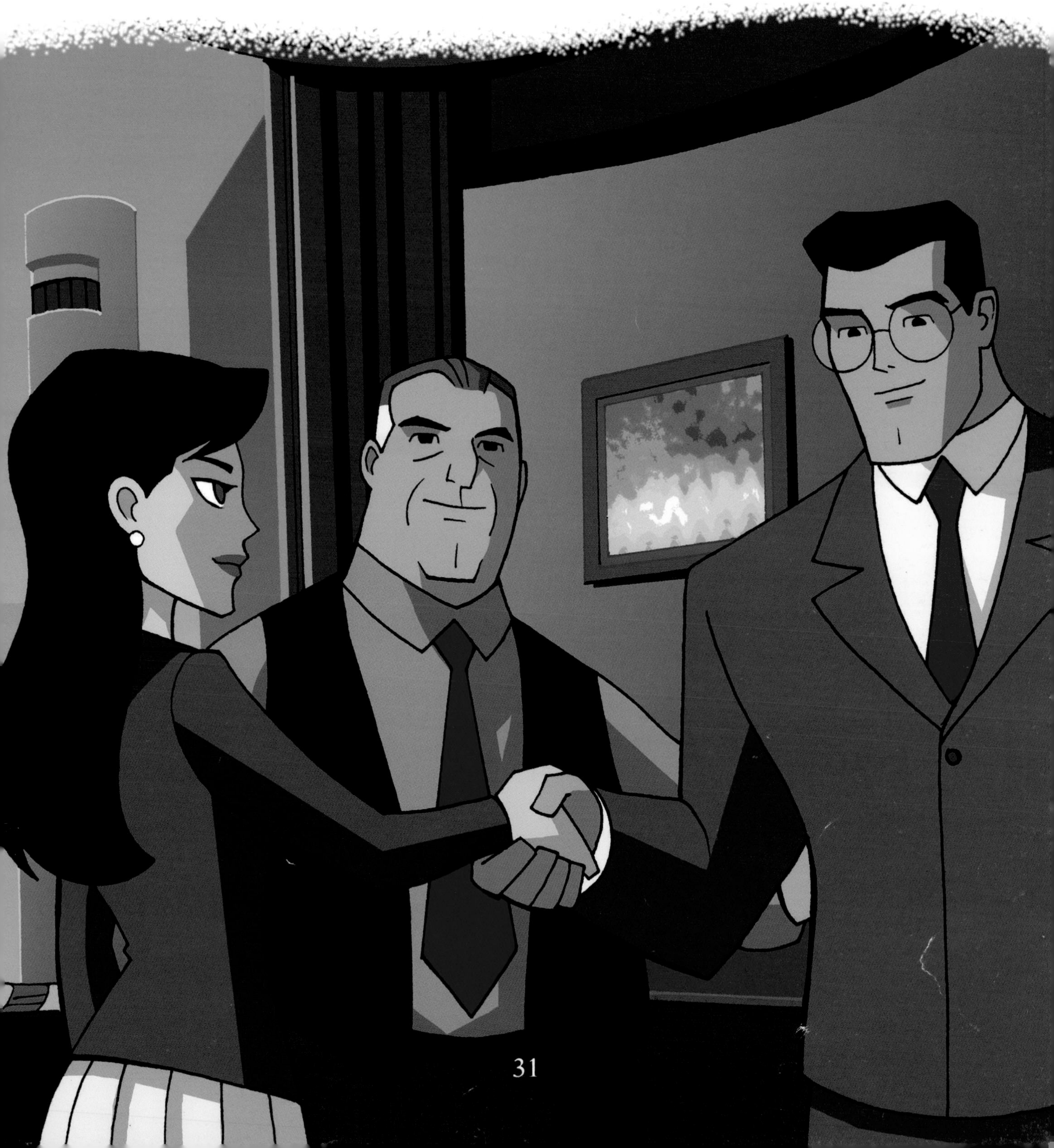

Before Clark knows it, he's trying his best to keep up with Lois.

Together, they go to cover a press conference for billionaire Lex Luthor. He reveals his new robot.

Clark knows all about Lex Luthor. Long before he moved to Metropolis, Clark had studied Lex's life.

The people of Metropolis think Luthor is a hero. But Clark knows better.

Lex is an evil billionaire. He will do anything to make money.

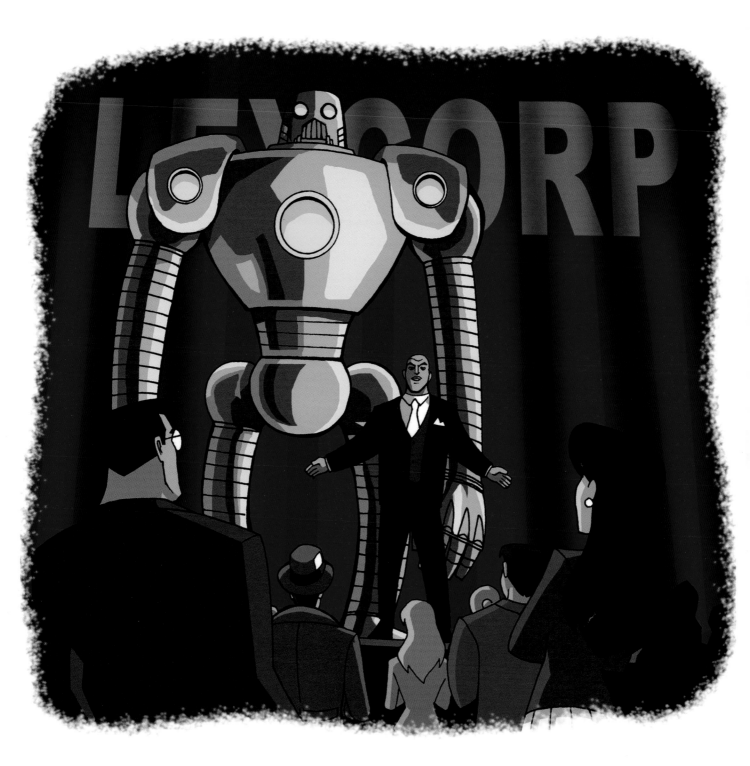

Suddenly Lex's giant robot malfunctions.

Luthor always tries to save money by cutting costs, so Clark isn't at all surprised.

The people in the crowd are too scared and busy to notice that Clark changes outfits.

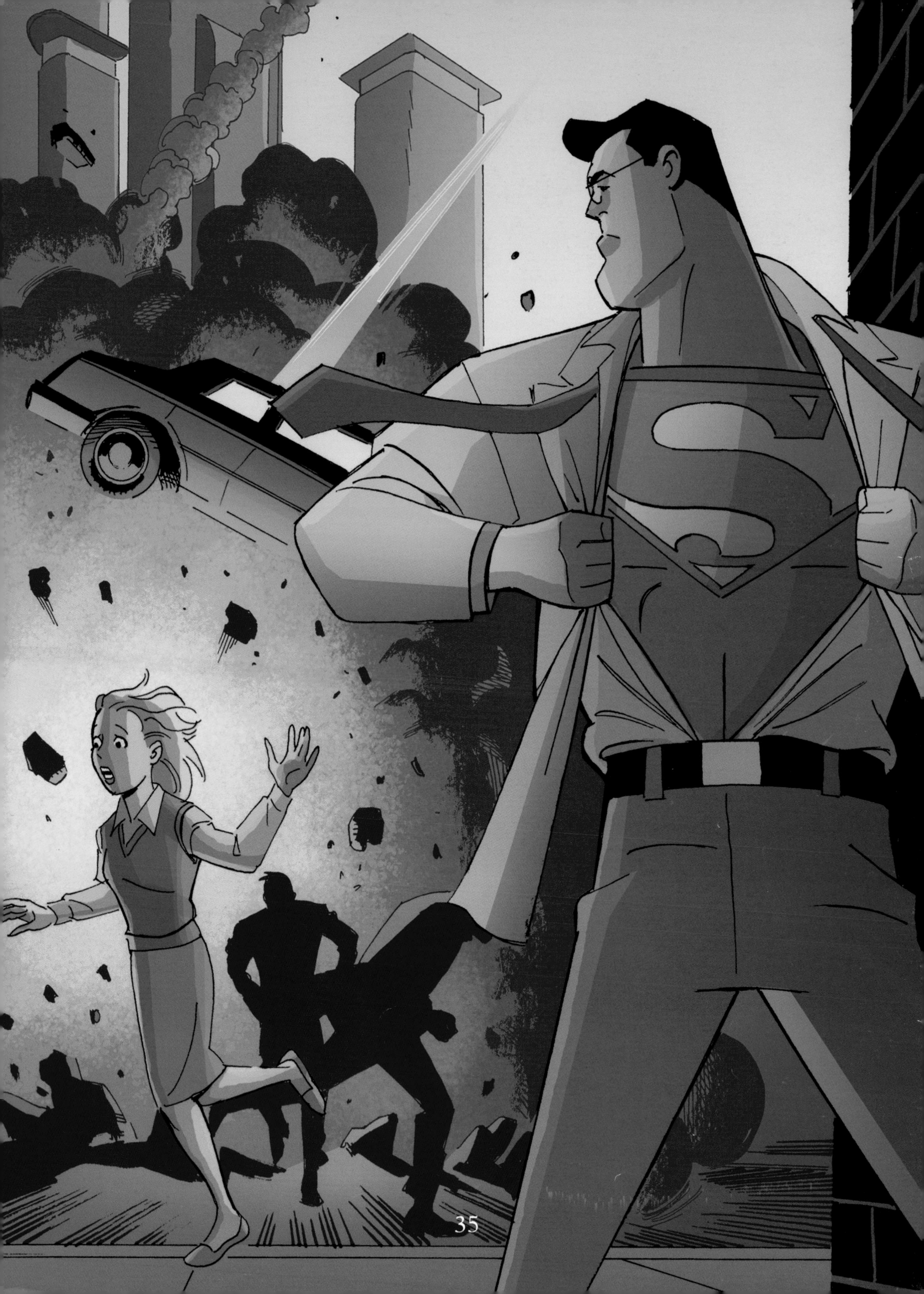

The robot tries to attack a redheaded young boy. But Clark saves him.

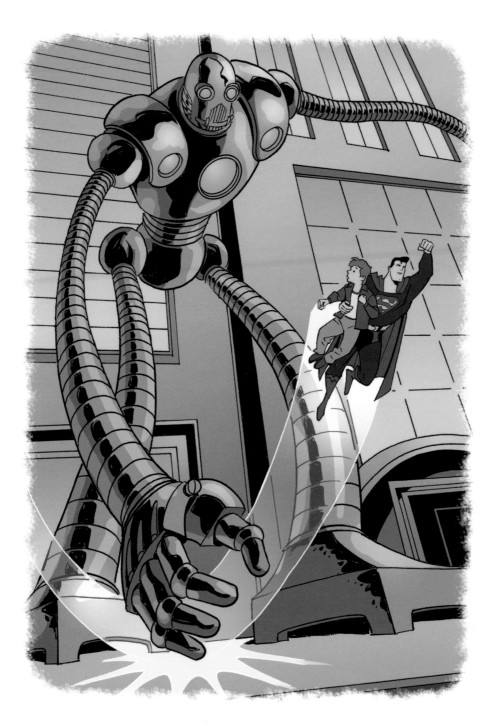

This is the moment Clark has prepared for all his life.

He has been sent to Earth to protect others.

Earth's yellow sun gives Clark's alien body extra energy.

He gains the powers of super-strength, super-speed, and invulnerability.

A metal robot doesn't stand a chance against the Man of Steel.

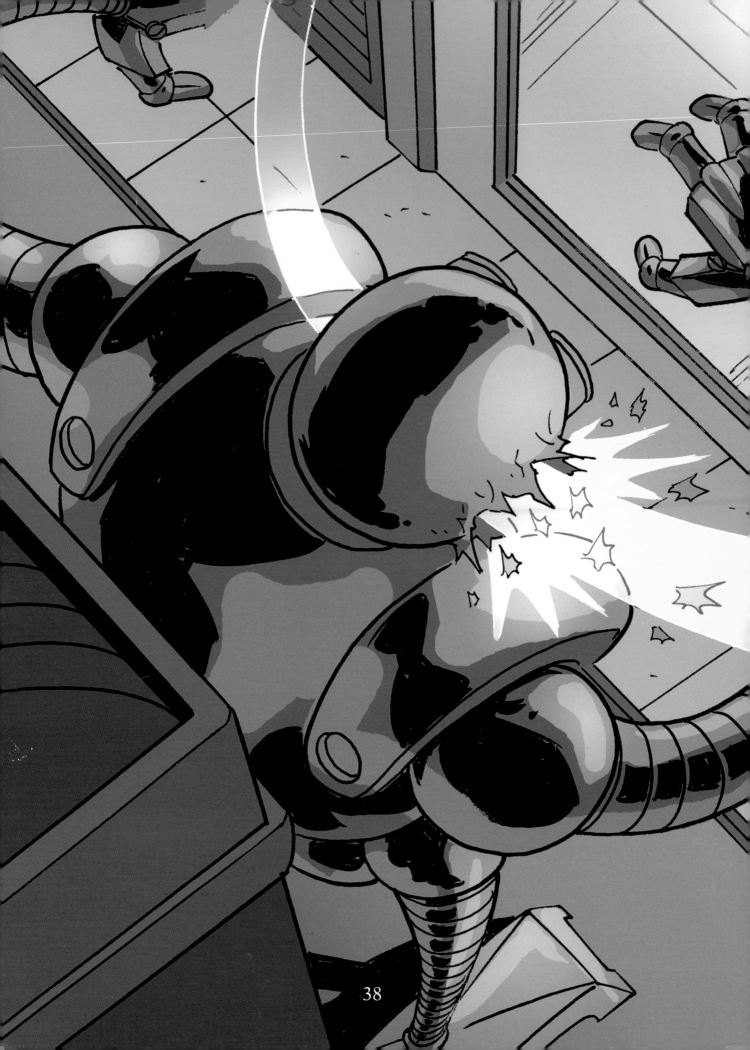

The redheaded boy snaps a photo of Superman in action.

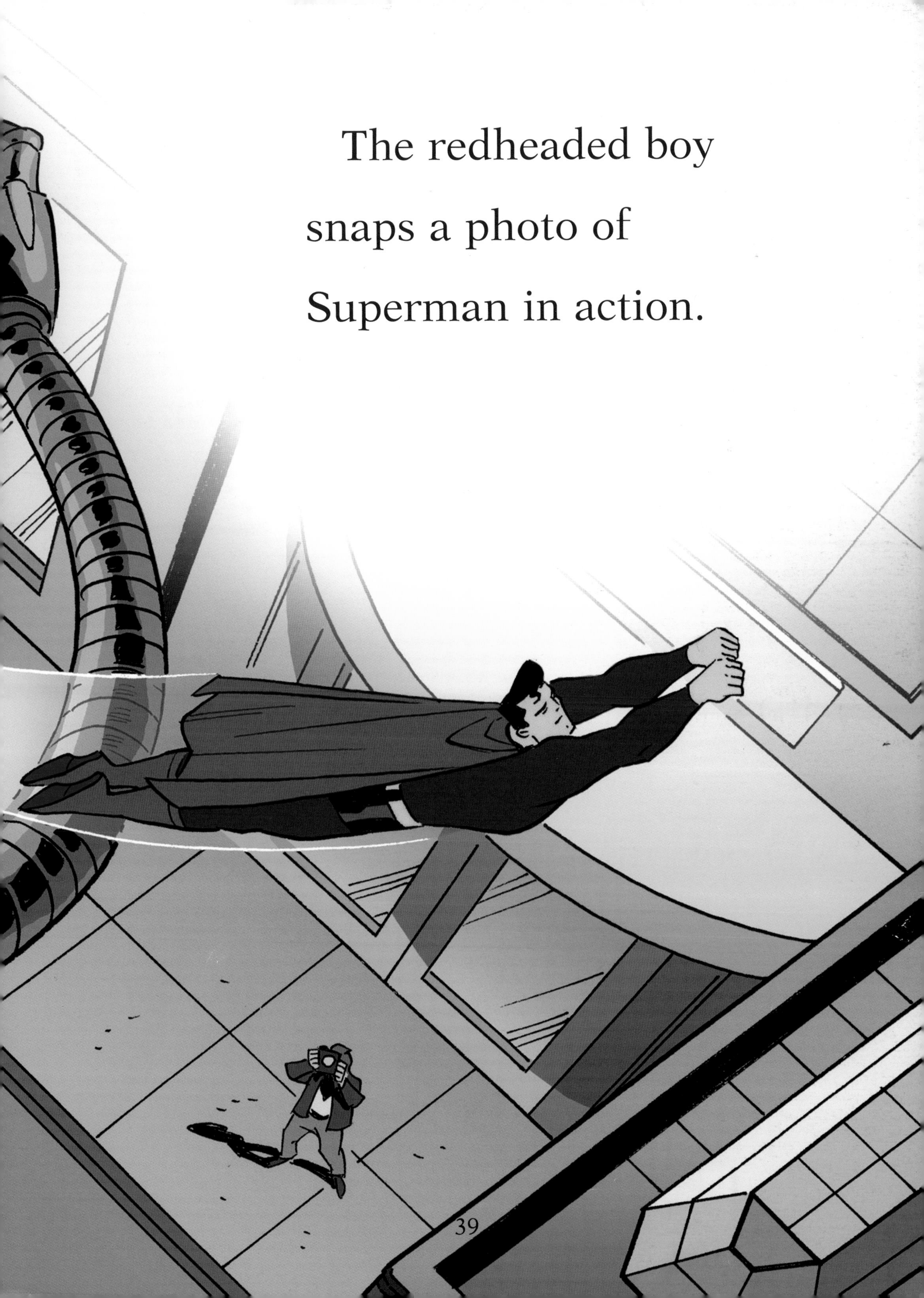

"Superman!" Lois Lane cries out. She is amazed by this new hero of Metropolis.

Clark smiles. Then he soars into the air.

He likes Lois very much. And he likes the name Superman, too.

Look, up in the sky!

It's a bird!

It's a plane!

It's Superman!

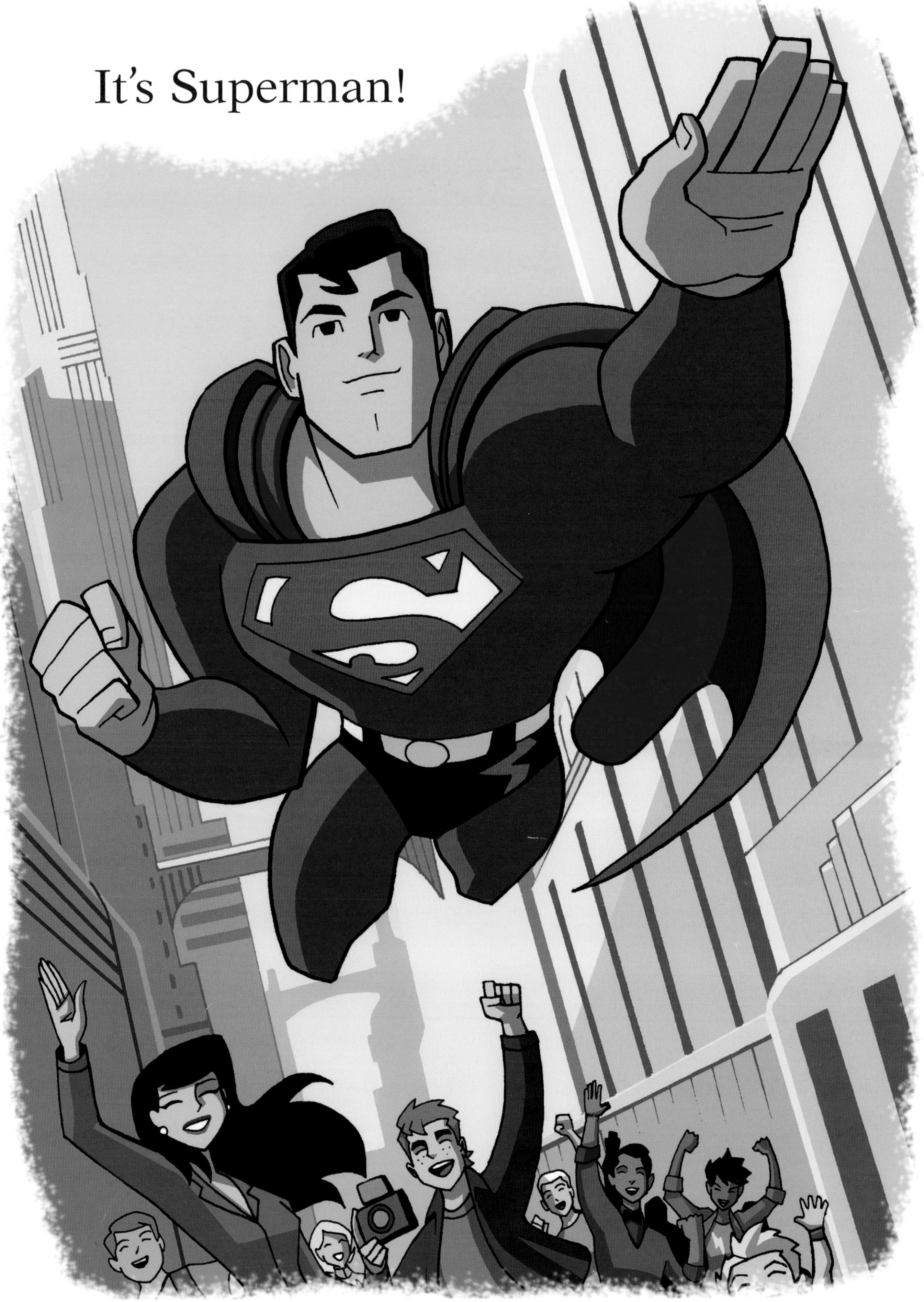

EVERYTHING ABOUT...

SUPERMAN™

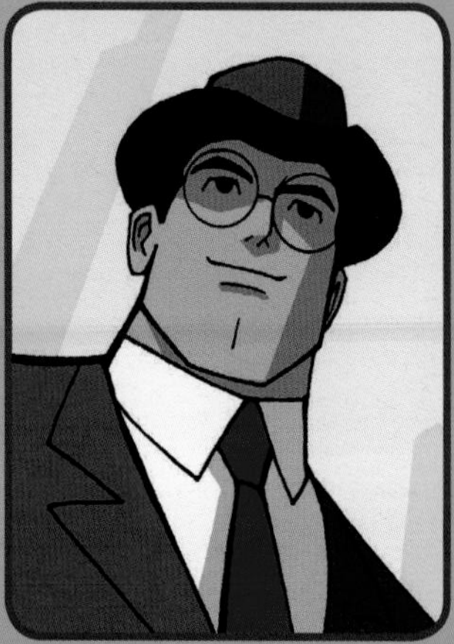

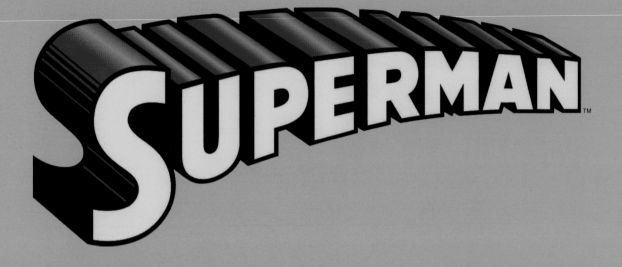

EARTH NAME: CLARK KENT

REAL NAME: KAL-EL

ROLE: PROTECTOR OF EARTH

BASE: METROPOLIS

Clark Kent is a mild-mannered reporter. The Man of Steel is the superpowered protector of Earth. While quite different on the outside, these two men are secretly the same person!

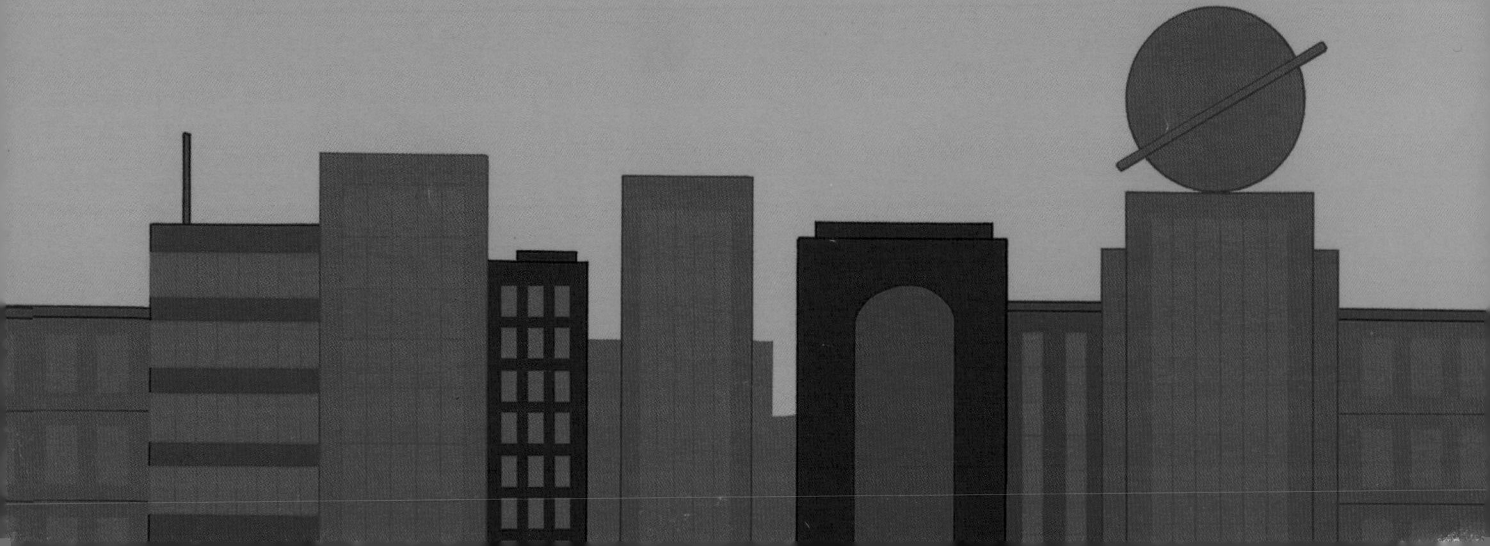

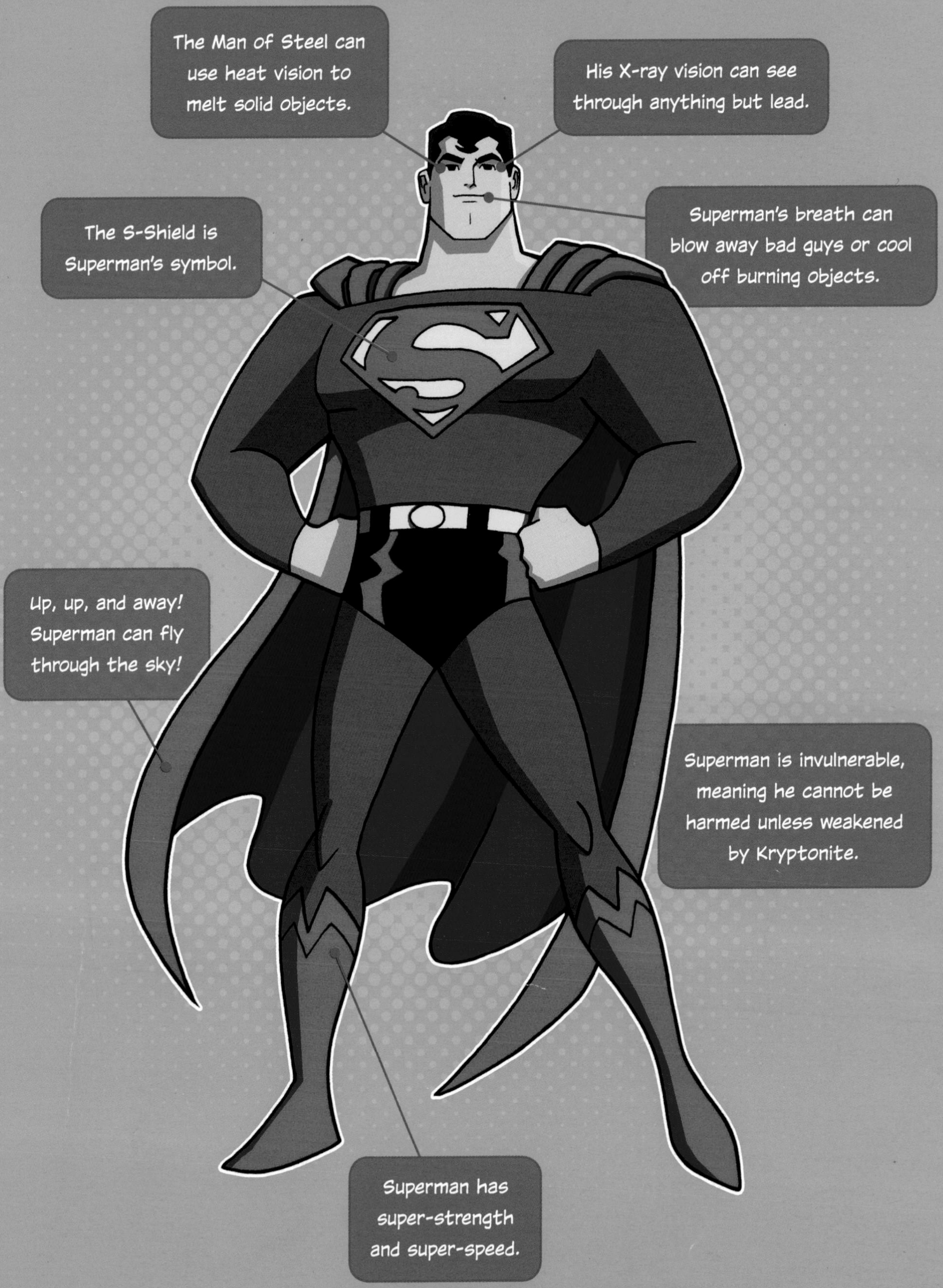
The Man of Steel can use heat vision to melt solid objects.
His X-ray vision can see through anything but lead.
The S-Shield is Superman's symbol.
Superman's breath can blow away bad guys or cool off burning objects.
Up, up, and away! Superman can fly through the sky!
Superman is invulnerable, meaning he cannot be harmed unless weakened by Kryptonite.
Superman has super-strength and super-speed.

THE AUTHOR

Over the course of **MATTHEW K. MANNING**'s writing career, he has written comics or books starring Batman, Superman, the Flash, the Justice League, and even Bugs Bunny. Some of his more recent works include the popular hardcover for Andrews McMeel Publishing entitled *The Batman Files*, a graphic novel retelling of *The Fall of the House of Usher*, and several DC Super Heroes books for Stone Arch Books. He lives in Mystic, Connecticut with his wife Dorothy and daughter Lillian.

THE ILLUSTRATOR

LUCIANO VECCHIO was born in 1982 and currently lives in Buenos Aires, Argentina. With experience in illustration, animation, and comics, his works have been published in the US, Spain, UK, France, and Argentina. His credits include Ben 10 (DC Comics), Cruel Thing (Norma), Unseen Tribe (Zuda Comics), and Sentinels (Drumfish Productions).

GLOSSARY

conductor (kuhn-DUHK-ter)—a person who collects tickets from passengers on a train or bus

device (di-VISSE)—an object, machine, or piece of equipment t made for some special purpose

fateful (FAYT-fuhl)—if something is fateful, it will be very important later on

infant (IN-fant)—a very young child

invulnerability (in-vuhl-nur-uh-BILL-i-tee)—unable to be harmed or damaged

malfunctions (mal-FUHNGK-shuhnz)—fails to work properly

realizes (REE-uh-lize-iz)—understands or becomes aware of something

recite (ri-SITE)—to read something out loud or say something from memory (usually for an audience)

reveals (ri-VEELZ)—shows something plainly or clearly, often for the first time

universe (YOO-nuh-verss)—all of space and everything in it including stars, planets, and galaxies

DISCUSSION QUESTIONS

Write down your answers. Refer back to the story for help.

QUESTION 1.

This illustration of Clark is on page 15. Based on how he looks in this shot, how do you think Clark feels? Why do you think he feels this way?

QUESTION 2.

On page 19, Jonathan and Martha Kent give Clark this device. Based on what you know about what happens next, what do you think this device is? What does it do?

QUESTION 3.

Who do you think this red-headed boy is? Why is he taking pictures of Superman?

QUESTION 4.

What clue did the illustrator leave for readers about who is inside this ship in this illustration?

Hint: it involves the rocket's path of travel.

READ THEM ALL!!

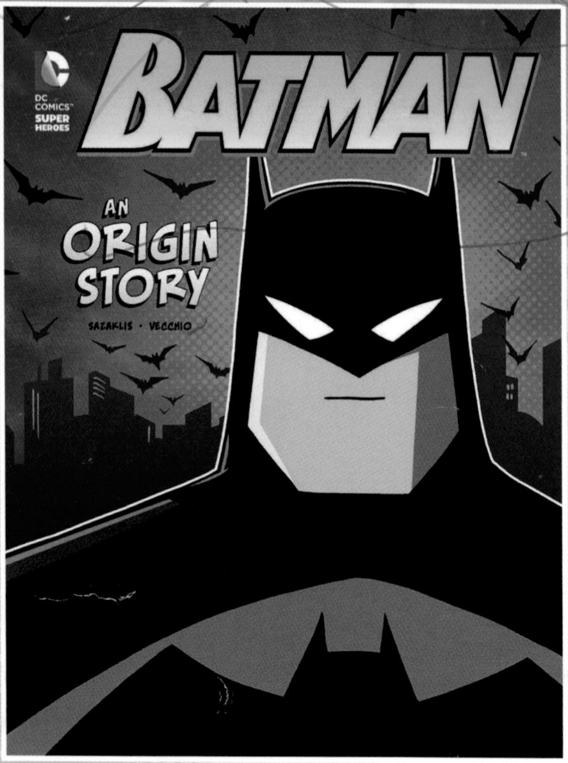

DC COMICS SUPER HEROES
BATMAN
AN ORIGIN STORY
SAZAKLIS • VECCHIO

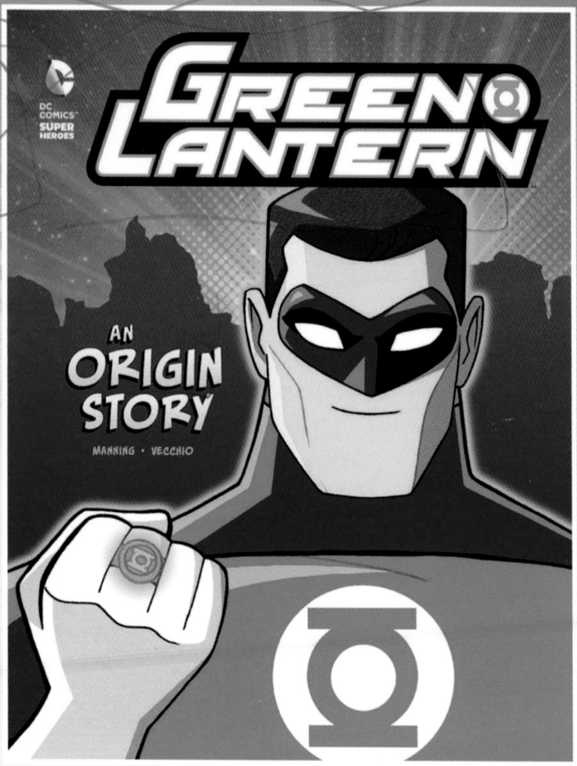

DC COMICS SUPER HEROES
GREEN LANTERN
AN ORIGIN STORY
MANNING • VECCHIO

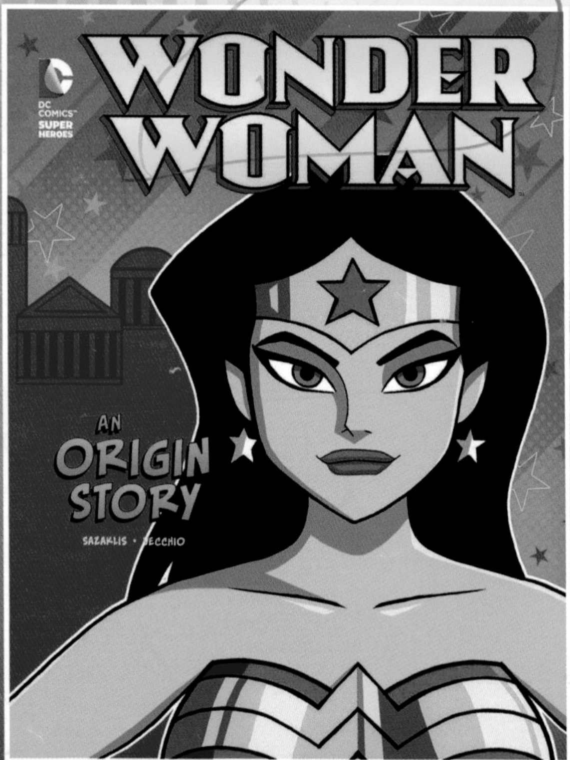

DC COMICS SUPER HEROES
WONDER WOMAN
AN ORIGIN STORY
SAZAKLIS • VECCHIO

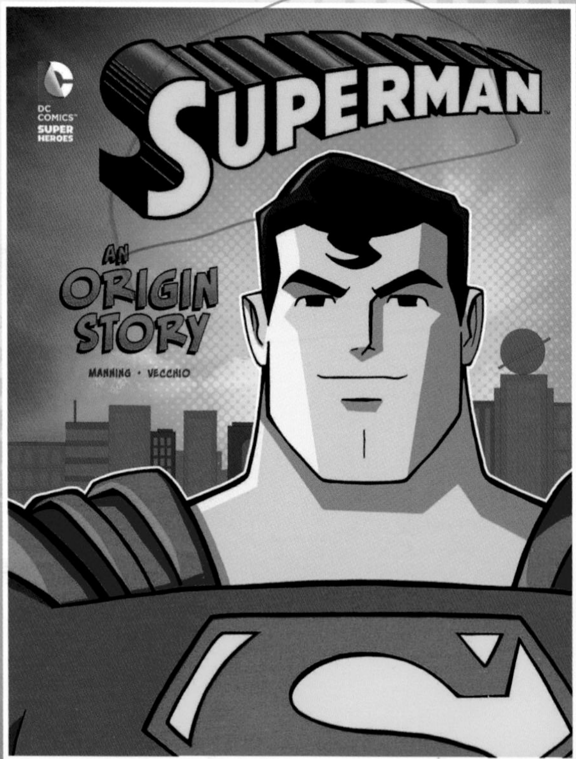

DC COMICS SUPER HEROES
SUPERMAN
AN ORIGIN STORY
MANNING • VECCHIO